# I Wish!

by Sue Graves

Illustrated by Shelagh McNicholas

W
FRANKLIN WATTS
LONDON • SYDNEY

I wish I were a butterfly with brown and orange wings.

I'd flutter round the garden, collecting nectar and sweet things.

But what if it got chilly?
A butterfly can't wear
a vest.

I'm glad I'm not a butterfly.
A butterfly is not the best!

11

I wish I were a horrid witch with a black and pointy hat.

I'd fly round on a
broomstick with Freddy,
my black cat.

15

But it's quite spooky late
at night.

There are bats and rats
and mice.

I'm glad I'm not
a horrid witch.
A witch is not so nice!

19

I wish I were a funny clown
with a red nose and a hat.

20

I'd play a lot of silly tricks
and flip like an acrobat.

23

# But custard pies get thrown at clowns!

They trickle down
your head!

I'm glad I'm not a funny clown, but what can I be instead?

It's hard to think of something that I would really like to be.

# And when I really think about it ...

# I'm very glad I'm me!

Leapfrog Rhyme Time has been specially designed to fit the requirements of the Literacy Framework. It offers real books for beginner readers by top authors and illustrators. There are 27 Leapfrog Rhyme Time stories to choose from:

## RHYME TIME

**Mr Spotty's Potty**
ISBN 978 0 7496 3831 3

**Eight Enormous Elephants**
ISBN 978 0 7496 4634 9

**Freddie's Fears**
ISBN 978 0 7496 4382 9

**Squeaky Clean**
ISBN 978 0 7496 6805 1

**Craig's Crocodile**
ISBN 978 0 7496 6806 8

**Felicity Floss: Tooth Fairy**
ISBN 978 0 7496 6807 5

**Captain Cool**
ISBN 978 0 7496 6808 2

**Monster Cake**
ISBN 978 0 7496 6809 9

**The Super Trolley Ride**
ISBN 978 0 7496 6810 5

**The Royal Jumble Sale**
ISBN 978 0 7496 6811 2

**But, Mum!**
ISBN 978 0 7496 6812 9

**Dan's Gran's Goat**
ISBN 978 0 7496 6814 3

**Lighthouse Mouse**
ISBN 978 0 7496 6815 0

**Big Bad Bart**
ISBN 978 0 7496 6816 7

**Ron's Race**
ISBN 978 0 7496 6817 4

**Woolly the Bully**
ISBN 978 0 7496 7098 6*
ISBN 978 0 7496 7790 9

**Boris the Spider**
ISBN 978 0 7496 7099 3*
ISBN 978 0 7496 7791 6

**Miss Polly's Seaside Brolly**
ISBN 978 0 7496 7100 6*
ISBN 978 0 7496 7792 3

**Juggling Joe**
ISBN 978 0 7496 7103 7*
ISBN 978 0 7496 7795 4

**What a Frog!**
ISBN 978 0 7496 7102 0*
ISBN 978 0 7496 7794 7

**The Lonely Pirate**
ISBN 978 0 7496 7101 3*
ISBN 978 0 7496 7793 0

**I Wish!**
ISBN 978 0 7496 7940 8*
ISBN 978 0 7496 7952 1

**Raindrop Bill**
ISBN 978 0 7496 7941 5*
ISBN 978 0 7496 7953 8

**Sir Otto**
ISBN 978 0 7496 7942 2*
ISBN 978 0 7496 7954 5

**Queen Rosie**
ISBN 978 0 7496 7943 9*
ISBN 978 0 7496 7955 2

**Giraffe's Good Game**
ISBN 978 0 7496 7944 6*
ISBN 978 0 7496 7956 9

**Miss Lupin's Motorbike**
ISBN 978 0 7496 7945 3*
ISBN 978 0 7496 7957 6

## Look out for Leapfrog
## FAIRY TALES

**Cinderella**
ISBN 978 0 7496 4228 0

**The Three Little Pigs**
ISBN 978 0 7496 4227 3

**Jack and the Beanstalk**
ISBN 978 0 7496 4229 7

**The Three Billy Goats Gruff**
ISBN 978 0 7496 4226 6

**Goldilocks and the Three Bears**
ISBN 978 0 7496 4225 9

**Little Red Riding Hood**
ISBN 978 0 7496 4224 2

**Rapunzel**
ISBN 978 0 7496 6159 5

**Snow White**
ISBN 978 0 7496 6161 8

**The Emperor's New Clothes**
ISBN 978 0 7496 6163 2

**The Pied Piper of Hamelin**
ISBN 978 0 7496 6164 9

**Hansel and Gretel**
ISBN 978 0 7496 6162 5

**The Sleeping Beauty**
ISBN 978 0 7496 6160 1

**Rumpelstiltskin**
ISBN 978 0 7496 6165 6

**The Ugly Duckling**
ISBN 978 0 7496 6166 3

**Puss in Boots**
ISBN 978 0 7496 6167 0

**The Frog Prince**
ISBN 978 0 7496 6168 7

**The Princess and the Pea**
ISBN 978 0 7496 6169 4

**Dick Whittington**
ISBN 978 0 7496 6170 0

**The Elves and the Shoemaker**
ISBN 978 0 7496 6581 4

**The Little Match Girl**
ISBN 978 0 7496 6582 1

**The Little Mermaid**
ISBN 978 0 7496 6583 8

**The Little Red Hen**
ISBN 978 0 7496 6585 2

**The Nightingale**
ISBN 978 0 7496 6586 9

**Thumbelina**
ISBN 978 0 7496 6587 6

**Other Leapfrog titles also available.**

* hardback